the SECRET ADVENTURES of CATS

WRITTEN AND ILLUSTRATED BY

Jacqueline Watson

1

the SECRET ADVENTURES of CATS

ISBN 978-1-7330940-1-6

The stories in this book are fiction,
and from the authors imagination.

I dedicate this book to all the people who have encouraged me to write, and to those who believed in my ability to draw. Also, I send a big thank you to Nora, who asked me to write a story about her cat, Tolula .... which gave me the idea to create this book.

Thank you so much xox

STORIES

TOLULA

Tolula is a pretty cat, although she doesn't like people telling her this. She thinks of herself more as a regal cat, especially as she rules the house she lives in.

Her fur is a tortoiseshell colour, and very soft and shiny. She has beautiful yellow eyes and a cute little black button nose.

She begins every morning by grooming herself. This is very important as Tolula likes to look her best for visitors when they come to see her.

Tolula lives with three little girls and their parents in a warm and cosy house …. and she has them all wrapped around her tiny paws.

One thing Tolula really doesn't like is to be cuddled; but she does like to be stroked.

No matter who she sits down next to, they know she wants to be stroked immediately. Without hesitation they do this, and only stop when Tolula gets up and walks away.

The door in Tolula's house does not have a cat flap set into it, like other cats have in their houses - I don't even think she knows what a cat flap is.

Tolula is a house cat, a stay in doors kind of cat, and she is more than happy with this. She has never been outside, and has never even tried to go outside, because everything she wants is inside her house.

Her food is given to her by a robot who delivers it at the same time everyday - and the robot is always on time. Tolula has tried to outsmart the robot on many occasions by sitting beside it at random times throughout the day and pawing at it. But the robot completely ignores her. It sticks to its duties and never fails to deliver the same exact amount of food at five, every afternoon.

Tolula's favourite pastime is to sit on her very tall cat perch which has been carefully positioned near the big front window of her house. She loves to sit here because she can see everything that goes on outside. She can see the garden, the long road in front of the house and the cars driving up her driveway just before they disappear into the garage, which is set underneath the main part of the house.

Tolula loves sitting on her cat perch, watching her girls playing on the lawn, and also when they ride their bikes up and down the quiet road in front of the house. Sometimes they will cycle too far up the road and Tolula loses sight of them. This causes her to panic slightly, and she will wave her tail from side to side watching intently until they come back into view.

On more than one occasion, Tolula has longed to be outside with her girls, especially when she hears them laughing and can see they are having so much fun. But Tolula is a house cat and knows better than to try and go near the front door of the house, which everyone uses to go out into the garden.

When Tolula wants peace and quiet she goes down the stairs into the basement. Down here there is a very large room where the girls play and their daddy watches a giant television. On the other side of this room is a smaller room. This is the laundry room, and is always nice and warm. This is Tolula's favourite room in the house and she loves to curl up and sleep on top of anything soft that is lying around in here.

Late one afternoon, just after Tolula had eaten her food delivered by her robot, she decided to take a nap. The family were busy working on something called homework at the dining-room table, and she never liked to disturb them during this time.

Quietly, Tolula went down the stairs into the basement and walked across the play room towards the laundry room. She noticed it didn't feel as warm down here as it usually did. In fact it felt a little chilly.

Tolula looked around and saw that the door leading into the garage was slightly ajar, which was very unusual as it was always tightly shut. Feeling curious, she squeezed through the gap and went into the garage. It felt even colder in here, and then Tolula realised why. The big garage door was wide open and she could see everything outside.

Tolula walked towards the open garage door and looked outside. She thought about going into the garden but hesitated, as she had never been outside of the house before. But the girls always looked like they were having fun out there, so maybe it wasn't that bad.

It was just starting to get a little dark and Tolula was still wondering what to do, when a mouse run past her and out into the garden.

Without thinking, Tolula ran outside after the mouse. The mouse ran as fast as he could with Tolula chasing close behind him.

The mouse ran up the road, took a left turn across some gardens, down another road, behind some shops, made a right turn out into the street and finally turned into a churchyard.

The mouse ran up the path to the church and then disappeared through a hole in the big wooden church door.

Tolula was not used to running, and running this far nearly took her breath away. Arriving at the church, she skidded to a halt just in time to see the mouse's tail disappear through the hole in the door.

Puffing slightly, Tolula wondered how she could get inside the church ... after all she hadn't run all this way just for fun. The hole the mouse had gone through was tiny, so that wasn't an option as Tolula was far too big to fit through there. The big wooden church door was firmly closed and the big round door handle was a long way from the ground. Even if Tolula could jump that high she would not be able to turn it.

Tolula looked around and decided to forget about the mouse and go back home. She had run a long way and that nap seemed even more appealing now. She walked down the path through the churchyard and into the street. Then she stopped.

Which way was home?

She had no idea where she was.

She had no idea which way she had come from.

This was the first time Tolula had ever been outside of her house and the mouse had led her all over the place.

What was she going to do?

It was getting quite dark now and Tolula felt a little scared.

What if she never finds her way home?

That would mean she would never see her three girls ever again.

And who would the robot feed each day?

Tolula decided to sit down and try to remember which way the mouse had led her. But no matter how hard she tried to think about this, it was all a blur. Her focus had been on catching the mouse, not on the direction she was running in.

All of a sudden Tolula heard a squeaking noise behind her. She turned around and saw the mouse running down the path from the church.

Tolula was too worried and upset to be bothered to chase the mouse again. So she just sat and continued trying to remember which way she had come from.

The mouse ran past Tolula and immediately turned left, and then ran up the street past the church.

Tolula just sat and watched him.

The mouse ran only a short way when he stopped, turned back and appeared to be looking right at Tolula.

Still Tolula just sat and watched him.

Then a strange thing happened.

The mouse ran back down the street to where Tolula was sitting, stopped right in front of her for a few seconds ....

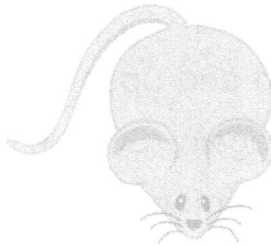

and then turned and ran back up the street in the same direction as he had just come from.

Then he stopped and looked back at Tolula as if to say, "Come on, follow me!"

Tolula decided to do this because she didn't know where else to run.

So she started running up to the mouse and the mouse started running away from Tolula. On and on they ran until eventually Tolula began to recognise her neighbourhood.

Very soon the mouse had led her back to her garden and there she saw her garage door.

BUT .....

..... it was closed.

The big garage door was shut tight.

OH NO!

What was Tolula going to do now?

Suddenly Tolula heard loud voices, and it sounded like the voices were shouting her name.

Looking up at the house, in the direction the voices were coming from, Tolula could see her three girls looking out of the big front window where her cat perch was. The three of them were looking straight at her, jumping up and down and shouting her name.

Tolula walked closer to the big window just as the girls' mummy opened the front door.

She came running outside and picked Tolula up, cuddling her tightly.

Tolula had never been so happy to have a cuddle and she snuggled in to the warm arms that squeezed her.

Tolula was home and she never wanted to go outside ever again.

The three girls were so happy to see her, and they all wanted to cuddle and stroke her at the same time. Tolula did not move away. She was really enjoying this.

Suddenly, Tolula heard the robot preparing her food. She was sure she had eaten before her adventure, but she ran over to it and gobbled up the food.

The girls' mummy had programmed the robot to give this special meal, as she was sure Tolula would be feeling very hungry after all that time out of the house.

Later that evening, after the girls had each given her a final cuddle and were tucked up in bed, Tolula went down to the basement for a well deserved sleep.

As she got closer to the laundry room, she glanced over at the door leading into the garage and saw it was still a little ajar. Tolula turned her back on this and continued into the laundry room where she found a warm and cosy spot to curl up in.

She thought about her crazy adventure and decided staying indoors and being a house cat was an excellent way to live.

She closed her eyes and was just starting to doze off when she heard a squeaking noise. Opening one eye, she saw the little mouse had curled up in a warm and cosy spot just opposite her.

Tolula smiled at the mouse and gave a contented sigh as she closed her eye again.

Just before she fell asleep, Tolula decided this little mouse was going to be a special friend because without him she felt sure she would still be wandering around outside in the dark.

Do you have a special friend?

LEO

"GET IT OUT!" shouts Leo's owner hysterically. Leo has just brought a mouse he has caught, into the house. He doesn't kill them; he catches them and then brings them home to play with. But for some reason his owner doesn't like this.

Leo has climbed in through the cat flap, with a tiny grey mouse in his mouth. Just as he is about to release it, his owner shrieks loudly. She opens the back door and kicks Leo out into the garden, slamming the door shut behind him.

Leo loves to hunt. It is his favourite thing to do, and every day he will hunt something. He hunts birds, mice, slugs and snails; in fact anything that moves. He doesn't mind how big or small his prey is, he just loves the thrill and excitement of lying in wait, and then pouncing just at the right moment to catch them.

Leo never kills anything he catches, although one time he thought he had killed a tiny bird.

The tiny bird had gone all limp and floppy in Leo's mouth as he was carrying it home. After climbing through the cat flap, Leo placed it carefully on the kitchen floor. The tiny bird was motionless. Leo pushed it gently with his paw a few times. All of a sudden, the bird started moving and flapping its wings. Leo was so happy it was still alive, but his owner was not so pleased, especially when the bird started pooping all over the floor.

Leo is a small ginger cat who may look weak, but is surprisingly strong and very agile. Leo has so much patience; he has been known to sit all night waiting for a mouse to come out of its hole. Nothing scares Leo, and even though he's a hunter, he has the kindest heart and loves helping anyone in distress.

Rain or shine, Leo wants to be outside. He wakes every morning as the sun rises, and eats a bowl of cat biscuits his owner leaves out for him. Then he steps out of the cat flap to explore and enjoy the day.

Just as the sun sets, Leo arrives back home feeling incredibly hungry. He climbs in through the cat flap and devours another bowl of biscuits his owner has put out for him. Then, totally exhausted after his busy day, he curls up somewhere warm and sleeps until the following morning.

This morning, after Leo has eaten his breakfast, he jumps through the cat flap and runs off to explore. He decides to go to a stream not far from his house, as he hasn't been there for a while. It's a sunny day and Leo runs along jumping up at the bugs which are flying around him.

It only takes a few minutes to get to the stream. But just as Leo is nearly there, he sees a big hairy dog running towards him. Leo quickly climbs a nearby tree and waits until the dog goes past.

Feeling sure that the coast is clear, Leo climbs down from the tree and continues walking closer to the stream. The grass is a little higher than normal and the bugs are enjoying the dandelion heads, which are in abundance.

Suddenly, Leo hears a squeaking sound coming from the stream. He peers into the water and sees a little mouse trying to clamber onto a floating leaf.

"Are you ok, little mouse?" Leo asks.

"Not really," splutters the little mouse, still trying to get a better grip onto the leaf. "Can you help get me out of here?"

Leo normally likes to catch mice for fun, but this mouse looks in need of help. "Yes, I'll help you," he says. Leo looks around to see how he can get the mouse out of the water, without getting wet himself.

The mouse is still holding onto the leaf with his tiny paws and floating up the stream. A little way ahead, Leo sees a large stick going from the grass bank into the stream. He runs up to the stick and carefully walks along it, just as the mouse floats under it. Crouching down, he manages to grab the mouse with his paw, and scoops him out of the water and onto the grass bank.

The mouse lies still for a moment and then splutters as some water falls out of his mouth.

"Are you all right?" asks Leo feeling a little concerned.

The mouse stands up carefully and says, "Yes, I think so."

"What were you doing in the water?" Leo asks curiously.

"I was running away from a big hairy monster and I didn't see the stream ahead of me ….. and just fell in," the mouse replies, feeling a little foolish. "Luckily the leaf floated next to me and I managed to grab hold of it."

"Well I think you should run home and stay safe for the rest of the day," Leo suggests.

"That's a good idea," says the mouse. "I don't think I have much energy in me to fight anything else today. Thanks for saving me." And he runs off before Leo can say another word.

Leo feels happy for the mouse and turns to look at the stream. There are lots of trees with low hanging branches almost dangling into the stream, and plenty of rocks lying haphazardly in the water. The stream is flowing slowly, and Leo watches a few leaves and twigs float by.

It is very quiet here. The only sounds Leo can hear are birds singing and some grasshoppers enjoying the sunshine nearby.

Unexpectedly, the peace is shattered as Leo hears a big SPLASH!

Leo turns around and can see a cat who has fallen into the stream.

"HELP ME! HELP ME!" she cries as she sloshes around in the water.

Leo runs over to the struggling cat.

What can he do to help? He doesn't like water, but he has to do something or this cat could drown.

"Stop struggling!" Leo shouts to the cat. "The current is moving you towards a tree branch. When you get there, reach up with your paws and grab the branch, then I will pull you to the bank."

A large rock near the bank is underneath this branch, and Leo runs over and stands on it, ready to pull the cat to safety.

The cat stops struggling and does what Leo has asked.

She reaches for the low hanging branch and grabs it between her paws. As quick as a flash, Leo grabs the cat and pulls her to the bank, where they both fall onto the grass in a heap.

"Are you ok?" asks Leo, as he stands up and looks at the wet cat.

The cat stands and shakes herself, and then starts to straighten her fur with her paw. She is a tiny cat, about half the size of Leo, and very pretty with blue eyes and white fur.

Shyly, she looks up at Leo, trying to hide her stare behind her long eyelashes. He is a handsome looking cat, she thinks to herself. "Thank you for rescuing me," she whispers nervously. "I slipped on one of the rocks and fell in. I must look a frightful mess." And she smooths her fur around her face.

Leo has never seen such a beautiful cat before and can't take his eyes off her. "You look gorgeous to me," he says, still taking in her beauty. "I am very pleased to have rescued you. My name is Leo, what's yours?"

"Lily," she says, thinking that it would be nice to spend more time with this charming cat.

"Would you like to walk with me for a while, Lily? The sun is still warm and will dry your fur." Leo thinks that spending some time with this beautiful cat will be very enjoyable.

"Yes please," Lily replies, feeling both excited and nervous at the same time.

This is the start of a new romance for Leo and Lily. Leo feels he has met the love of his life, and now has a companion he never realised he needed.

Leo never goes hunting again, and never brings mice or birds in through the cat flap; he only brings his new girlfriend home, which his owner is very happy about.

Have you ever had to rescue an animal from a stream?

MIMI

"Have you seen Mimi today?" asked Mrs M as she gazed out of the kitchen window.

"Not since breakfast this morning," replied her husband, looking up from his newspaper.

"It's getting late and she hasn't been home for her tea," Mrs M said, as she started to feel a little anxious about her precious cat. "It's not like her to be out for so long. She's always home at four thirty on the dot and it's just after five thirty now. I hope she's okay."

"I'm sure she is," replied her husband, going over and putting his arm around his wife's shoulders. "You know how friendly she is. I expect she's curled up on Sally's lap, two doors down."

"But Sally normally sends her home after four; and it rained this afternoon - Mimi always comes home when it rains." Mrs M was getting more and more worried.

"Stop over thinking things," her husband said gently as he pulled her into his arms. "You are getting yourself upset for nothing. If she's not home in half an hour I'll go and find her."

Mimi was an extremely friendly cat who loved everyone, and believed everyone loved her too. Snuggling up on a warm lap was the perfect place for her, and she didn't mind whose lap it was. She loved to be made a fuss of, and would spend all day purring, as long as she was being stroked by somebody.

Everyone who lived in her neighbourhood really did love Mimi, and would always stop and talk to her as she passed by. Often they would take the time to bend down and make a fuss of her, while telling her what a beautiful cat she was.

Actually, did I say everyone loved Mimi?

Well, everyone did love Mimi until last Tuesday when Mrs B moved out of her house and Mr D moved in.

Mrs B always welcomed Mimi into her house and would feed her a tin of tuna. Mrs B did not like tuna but she would buy it just for Mimi's visits.

Most days, around lunchtime, Mimi would climb over Mrs B's back fence, jump down into the garden and go to the backdoor. If she couldn't attract Mrs B's attention by standing at the backdoor, she would leap up and swing on the door handle. This made such a noise when Mimi's paws slipped off and the handle pinged back into place. Mimi would keep doing this until Mrs B opened the door and let her in.

Last Tuesday Mrs B moved to a different neighbourhood, and an elderly gentleman called Mr D moved into her house.

Mr D did not like cats at all. He thought they were the worst creatures on earth. You see, Mr D used to keep pigeons and the local ginger tom cat, who was an extremely large ginger tom cat, would chase Mr D's pigeons day and night. Mr D would scream and shout, but the ginger tom cat

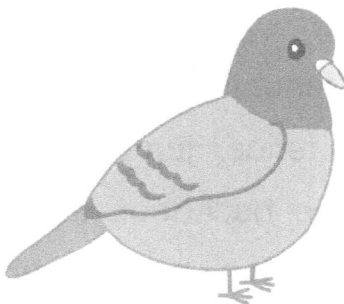

was not scared of him, and would continue to chase the pigeons every chance he could.

Mr D became so angry that all the children in his neighbourhood wouldn't play near his house. The shouting really scared them. Their mums complained about Mr D's bad language but this didn't stop him. Soon nobody in his neighbourhood liked him and would ignore him if they saw him out walking.

Before too long the ginger tom cat had either frightened all the pigeons away or killed them; and so Mr D decided to move houses, away from the bad memories he had of this neighbourhood.

This particular day Mr D was busy in the lounge, unpacking the last of his boxes, when he heard a weird noise at his backdoor. He wasn't a very curious man and decided to ignore it. A few seconds later he heard the noise again …. and again.

Mr D began to feel very annoyed by this disruption, and stopped what he was doing to go and take a look.

He flung open the backdoor …. and there was nobody there.

This annoyed Mr D even more.

Just as he was about to shut the door, he heard a cat meow. He looked down at the same moment as Mimi brushed past his legs and went into the kitchen, as if she lived there.

"What the blazes do you think you are doing?" shouted Mr D, picking up Mimi and throwing her into the garden. "Get out and stay out!" he bellowed as he slammed the door shut; and he stomped back to his boxes, extremely irritated.

Mimi felt a bit discombobulated after being thrown from such a great height. And who was that angry old man in Mrs B's kitchen?

Mimi stood up and stretched her body which helped her feel a little better. She walked over to the backdoor and jumped up at the handle a few times. She was not one to give up on something, and she knew there was always a delicious tin of tuna in that house.

This time Mr D opened the kitchen window and yelled loudly at Mimi, "Clear off, you mangy cat, before I come out there and string you up!" And he banged the window shut before going back into the lounge.

Mimi climbed onto the window ledge and looked through the kitchen window. Where had he gone? The old man was nowhere to be seen. And where was Mrs B?

Mimi was used to getting her own way. People liked her and would go out of their way to be kind to her. She was not comfortable with someone being mean to her.

Mimi started to claw at the window, when suddenly the old man came running into the kitchen. He was waving his arms franticly above his head and hollering so loudly that Mimi slipped off the ledge with fright ... and fell into the flowerbed.

Mimi lay there for a few seconds and then stood up and cleaned the dirt off her fur. She decided to have one more try at getting the old man's attention.

She went over to the backdoor and jumped up at the handle a few times.

As she landed on the ground for the third time the backdoor flew open taking her by surprise, and the old man threw a bucket of cold water all over her. "How many times have I got to tell you to go away?" he screamed. "Here, maybe this will help you get the message," and he threw his boot at Mimi.

Dripping wet, Mimi started to run up the garden just as the boot hit her on her back ..... BOOM .... and knocked her to the ground.

The boot had knocked the wind out of Mimi, and she lay on the ground motionless.

"Clear off I say!" shouted Mr D.

But Mimi did not move.

"Don't make me come over there!" he shouted again.

Still Mimi did not move.

Mr D hesitated wondering what to do next. Had he killed the cat? He didn't like cats, but deep down he wouldn't hurt them.

He was about to go back into his house when he heard a slight murmur coming from the cat. Slowly he walked over and could see that he hadn't injured the cat, apart from winding it. He felt bad about this but didn't know what he could do. It was beginning to rain a little so he couldn't leave the cat outside.

Mr D went into his house and found an old towel he had used for his pigeons. He grabbed it and went back out into the garden. Very gently he picked up the cat and wrapped her in the towel, then carried her indoors.

He went into the lounge where he had been unpacking boxes, and laid Mimi inside one of the empty boxes. He thought this would keep her warm and safe until she woke up.

Mr D sat and watched the cat. He thought how tiny and fragile she looked, and felt really upset with his actions. He used to be a friendly man who loved people and animals. But he had become lonely when his wife died, and his pigeons had been his only friends. He had turned into a grumpy old man when the ginger tom cat began to stalk his birds. Maybe he should have befriended the tom cat instead of being angry towards it; maybe things would have been different then.

As he looked at Mimi a tear came into his eye. His wife would have been very disappointed with the way he had behaved. The thought of this made him feel quite upset. He needed to change his ways, and decided today he would start to be kind to people and animals again. He would begin by being kind to this sweet little cat in his box.

But first she must wake up.

Mr D didn't have long to wait because as soon as Mimi had warmed up, she opened her eyes. She looked up out of the box and saw the old man staring down at her.

Mimi purred.

"Hey, old girl, are you feeling better?" Mr D asked in the softest voice he could.

Mimi purred again.

"I'm sorry I threw that boot at you. I never meant for it to hit you, I only wanted to scare you."

Mimi purred again.

Mr D went into the kitchen and came back with a saucer of milk, which he placed on the floor. He gently lifted Mimi out of the cardboard box and stood her next to the saucer.

"Here, drink this. It will help you feel better."

Mimi wobbled slightly but soon got her balance and purred before she took a drink of the milk. It was deliciously cold and creamy. Mimi looked up at the old man and purred again, then she lapped up the rest of the milk.

After wiping her whiskers with her paw, she went up to the old man and brushed around his legs, in and out, purring loudly.

"You're not a bad old cat are you?" said Mr D, pleased that she was okay. He bent down and stroked her. Mimi purred louder. "You like that then uhh?" Mimi purred in reply.

"I wonder who you belong to," said Mr D. "You've been here most of the day. I expect your owner may be getting worried." He noticed that Mimi was wearing a tiny pink cat collar which had a small silver coloured disc dangling from it.

"Come over here, I need to find my specs. I can't read anything without them." The old man went over to the sofa and sat down, grabbing his glasses which were on a small table next to the sofa. Mimi jumped up onto the sofa next to Mr D, and stepped upon his lap.

The old man held the disc on Mimi's collar and read, "Mimi - 752 368 1141"

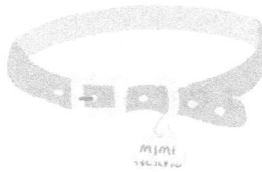

"Mimi. That's a cute name," he said stroking her head and smiling. "Well Mimi, I should call your owner. Move off my lap and I'll go and ring that number," and he gently nudged her. But Mimi had other ideas, and curled up in a ball on Mr D's lap and fell fast asleep.

"Oh well, I'm sure five minutes won't hurt," he said looking at the contented cat.

Sitting on the sofa, stroking the warm cat on his lap, Mr D was the most relaxed he had been in years. Before too long, he nodded off himself.

Mimi was the first to wake, and as she stood up to stretch, Mr D opened his eyes.

It was dark in the house.

"Oh no, what time is it?" He looked at his watch. It was just coming up to six o'clock.

Mimi jumped onto the floor and Mr D quickly stood up.

"Let me call the number on your collar," he said as he walked into the kitchen to use the phone. He dialed the number and a lady answered, "Hello."

"Hello, my name is Mr D and I have a pretty little tortoiseshell cat here called Mimi. Would she belong to you?"

"Oh yes," came the reply. "Mimi belongs to us, Mr and Mrs M. We were just wondering where she had got to."

"If you give me your address, I will bring her home," Mr D replied, not really wanting to get into a conversation about the events of the day.

Mrs M told Mr D her address.

"Oh!" he exclaimed. "You are just over the road from my house."

"Are you the new owner of Mrs B's house?" Mrs M asked.

"Yes I am," Mr D answered.

"That explains why Mimi is with you," replied Mrs M with a smile on her face. "Mrs B always fed her a tin of tuna when Mimi went over there. I'm sorry if she's been a nuisance. She really loves people and thinks everybody loves her."

"She has been no trouble at all," said Mr D, bending down and stroking Mimi as she brushed against his legs, purring. "She has made a friend in me …. I can understand why everybody loves her. I'll bring her straight home now."

Mr D said goodbye and picked Mimi up, giving her a cuddle.

"I'm sorry for our misunderstanding today, old girl, but I am very pleased you came to visit me. You've helped me to realise that not all cats are naughty, and the way I treat anyone is the way they will treat me. The next time you come over to visit me, I will have a tin of tuna waiting for you."

Mimi nuzzled into Mr D's neck, as if she understood every word he had said.

Do you think your pet understands everything you say?

ROCKET

ZOOM!　　Rocket ran around so fast you would only catch a glimpse of fur as the cat ran up the stairs, down the stairs, and round and round the house.

Being as fast as a rocket, Rocket hardly ever sat still, and certainly suited the name. Even at night when the house was fast asleep, Rocket would hear a noise and be off, looking for what was causing it.

Rocket was a very fluffy forest cat with long smokey grey fur and a white lion's mane. Rocket lived on the edge of a big forest with two boys, who could always find lots of places to have fun and explore.

Rocket was happy and loved. But things had not always been this good. Settling down to rest one evening, Rocket remembered when life was so much different ....

"GET THAT DARN CAT OUT OF HERE!" shouted the grumpy lady, with a cigarette hanging out of the side of her mouth. "I DON'T want to see it in this house EVER again."

"But Mum, I love Rocket," whispered the little girl, holding her cat tightly.

"Don't argue with me, child. Do as I tell you AND GET IT OUT!"

The little girl reluctantly carried Rocket outside. She bent down and placed the sad cat onto the street. Stroking Rocket's head she said, "I'm sorry Rocket but I have to do what my mum says. She has never liked cats. I knew that when I brought you home, but I thought she would let you stay, as you're so cute." Standing up, the little girl looked down at her adorable cat. "Goodbye Rocket, I hope you find a new home soon with someone who will love you as much as I do." The little girl went back into the house and, after one last look at Rocket, she closed the door.

Rocket walked away from the house and headed towards the forest, which was not far from this neighbourhood. Life had not been easy for this poor cat but surely that had to change soon.

As Rocket started walking into the forest, a voice said, "Hello!" Rocket looked around wondering who was speaking.

"I'm over here by the fallen tree," said the voice.

Rocket looked over towards the fallen tree and saw a large white cat peeking over it.

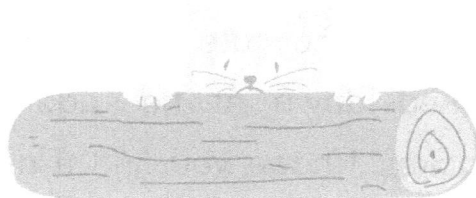

Rocket walked nearer to the white cat. "Hello," said Rocket. " What are you doing?"

The white cat jumped up onto the fallen tree and looked down at Rocket. "I'm looking for something fun to do. What are you doing?"

Rocket gazed up at the white cat and thought how big he looked. "I've just been kicked out of my home. The lady who lives there doesn't like cats and told the little girl, who seemed to love me, to get rid of me."

"That's a mean thing to do," the white cat said as he jumped off the fallen tree and stood next to Rocket.

"Yes, I think so too. But it's not the first time I've lost my home," Rocket said sadly. "I used to live with lots of other cats in a big house where I was born. An old lady who looked after us called me Rocket one day when I was running around the house so fast as I tried to get away from a big black cat. He was a bully and used to boss all the cats around. Anyway, I wouldn't put up with that so he would chase me. I just ran as fast as I could until he got tired. Then he would fall asleep for hours and leave me and all the other cats alone."

"So why couldn't you stay there?" the white cat asked, sitting down in front of Rocket.

Rocket sat down too and replied, "One day, the old lady fell over some of the kittens and broke something. She was in a lot of pain, and people came and took her away to make her better. Well, they left the door wide open and lots of the cats ran outside, and I followed them. They ran in different directions and suddenly I was all alone. I wandered around the streets and a little boy found me. He took me home with him, but his dad didn't want a smelly cat in the house. That night, when the boy was asleep, the man drove me to a park and threw me out of the car ..... that's where the little girl found me."

"Oh that's so sad," the white cat said, thankful that he lived with a loving family.

"Yes, I suppose it is," Rocket said thinking about it. "But it was fun living with all the cats, even though some of them were not very nice at times."

"Well, I'm very pleased to meet you, Rocket. My name is Steven. I live just down the road, but I come up here to play in the forest. Come on, let's go and have some fun." The new friends started walking deeper amongst the trees.

"What's the highest tree you've ever climbed?" asked Steven.

"I've never climbed a tree before," Rocket said, looking around and thinking that he had never seen such tall trees up to now.

"What!" exclaimed Steven. "A boy cat who has never climbed a tree before. Well, we have to change that right this minute. I'll race you up that tree over there." And Steven ran ahead and straight up the trunk of the biggest tree Rocket had ever seen. "Come on, Rocket, you're so slow. I'm nearly at the top. I thought you were fast at everything you do."

"I am!" answered Rocket, carefully climbing the tree. "This is my first time climbing. Next time I'll be so fast you won't see me for dust." Rocket reached a branch near Steven. "Wow, what a great view up here," Rocket said looking around.

"Yes," said Steven. "You can see everything up here. I often climb a tree just to look at what's going on in the forest below."

"Wait!" exclaimed Rocket. "Did you hear that noise?" They listened. The sounds of rustling leaves and twigs being snapped could be heard.

Steven looked around. "Oh no," he said. "I can see a big bear coming straight towards us. Good thing we're up in this tree out of his way. Stay still and he won't know we're here."

The cats watched as the bear stopped at the bottom of the tree they were hiding in. He looked around and started sniffing the air with his big bear nose.

Rocket looked at Steven, feeling very scared. The bear was so huge, the biggest animal Rocket had ever seen.

The bear looked up into the tree. "It's no good hiding, I can still smell you," he said in a big gruff voice.

"We aren't hiding," said Steven, still hiding amongst the leaves on the tree.

"What are you doing then?" asked the bear as he started to push the tree with his paws. "I can't see you."

Steven went to answer the bear, but Rocket tried to tell him to be quiet.

Steven took no notice of Rocket and said to the bear, "We are looking for food."

"Ohhh, so there's two of you up there," the bear growled, seemingly frustrated that he couldn't see the animals.

"Yes, I'm here with my friend Rocket," Steven announced.

Rocket was flabbergasted that Steven was sharing such information, and nearly fell out of the tree in shock.

The bear walked his paws up the tree and started pushing the leaves apart, as he searched for his prey.

Unexpectedly, Steven winked at Rocket and then jumped down from the tree, landing on the bears big nose. This took the bear by surprise, and he fell backwards as he grabbed the cat between his large paws.

"Hey, not so tight," squealed Steven.

"Oh I'm sorry," apologised the bear, letting go of Steven and sitting up.

Rocket watched all this from up in the tree and wondered what was happening. Why hadn't the bear eaten Steven? Puzzled, Rocket continued watching, from the safety of the tree.

"You don't know your own strength, Berty," said Steven laughing. "Give me a gentle bear hug."

To Rockets astonishment, Berty the bear gave Steven a very gentle bear hug.

After a minute, Berty let the cat go and asked, "So who's your friend then, Steven?"

Steven looked up at the tree and shouted, "Come down, Rocket. Berty won't hurt you. He's a big soft teddybear."

Noticing that Steven was not at all scared by the bear, Rocket very carefully climbed down the tree.

"Hello," said Berty in as gentle a voice as he could, so as not to scare Rocket. "Any friend of Steven's is a friend of mine. Nice to meet you."

"Hello, n..n..nice to meet you too, I think," stammered Rocket, feeling only slightly nervous now.

"Berty and I have been friends for years," Steven explained. "One day he saved me from a very angry and hungry wolf, which I'll be forever grateful for. Sorry we tricked you, Rocket."

"That's ok, I wasn't scared at all!" Rocket answered, hoping he sounded convincing.

"Well, I haven't got time to chat today," said Berty. "I need to get going. I hope to see you both again soon and we can for chat longer then." The cats said goodbye and watched Berty the bear as he walked away, deeper into the forest.

"I should be getting home too," said Steven. "What are you going to do?" he asked Rocket.

"Oh, I'll be fine here for a while," answered Rocket, looking around for a spot to rest in. "I don't feel too good at the moment. I think maybe tree climbing is not for me. I'll just lie down here for a few minutes and take a nap."

"Hopefully you will feel better after that," said Steven, feeling slightly concerned. "Are you sure you'll be ok on your own?"

"Yes, I'm sure," said Rocket, curling up on a pile of leaves under a tree. "I just need some rest. You go and I'll see you another day."

Steven slowly walked off but looked back a few times, until eventually he couldn't see Rocket anymore.

Rocket had unusual tummy pains, but was convinced they would pass after a sleep.

Climbing up and down that tree was hard work, even for a cat.

As Rocket slept, he dreamt about being loved and cared for, when suddenly the dream was interrupted by a noise. Rocket looked up and saw two faces staring down at him.

"He's alive mum, he's alive!" two boys shouted together. "Can we take him home, mum, please? He looks so sad and lonely."

"Yes we can," their mum said, taking a closer look at the cat. "He doesn't look very well, though. Maybe some warmth and food will help. But you can't keep him as he may belong to someone. Let's get him home and I'll start to ask around."

"Look mum, he's wearing a collar with a metal disc on it!" exclaimed the eldest boy. He read the words on the disc, "*MY NAME IS ROCKET*. That's a great name for a boy, mum, don't you think?"

"Yes it is," she replied, hoping he wouldn't get too attached to the cat.

The boys took turns to carry the cat home, and then fed him some warm milk. After drinking a mouthful or two, Rocket wandered off to explore the house. The boys started to follow, but their mum said, "Leave him go. He looks exhausted and probably just needs to adjust to being here. Now don't get too attached to him. I've put a message out on social media and informed the local vets, so someone could claim him at anytime."

"He's such a cute cat, mum," said the youngest boy.

"I know," she replied gently. "We'll get a cat one day. Now, why don't you and your brother watch some TV for a while before dinner?"

The house was quiet except for the sound of the television.

"Meow, meow ….."

"That's Rocket!" said the eldest boy. "I wonder what's wrong?"

"Let's go and find out," said his mum. And the three of them went to find the cat.

"Mum, Rocket's in here," announced the youngest boy. "Look!" and he pointed to the floor by the bottom of his bed.

Rocket was curled up on some dirty clothes, looking up at the boy. But Rocket was not alone ….. there were two little kittens there too!

So Rocket was not a boy cat after all, but a cute little girl cat.

Nobody came forward to claim Rocket, so the boys adopted him … sorry, I should say her. Also, after some gentle persuasion and promising to always do their homework on time, the boys convinced their mum to keep the kittens.

They all lived happily together and spent many hours exploring and having fun in the forest. Steven joined them most days and even Berty the bear paid a visit now and again.

Rocket had all the love and attention she had only ever dreamt about before, and was thankful everyday for her wonderful life with her very special family.

Would you be scared if you saw a bear in the forest? If you did see a bear, what would you do?

SPARKLE

If you have never seen a cat who should have been a princess, then you need to meet Sparkle.

Sparkle is an extremely glamorous looking cat. She is very spoilt and loves nothing more than to sit and preen herself with elaborate care for hours every day.

Her name suits her because her fur is so well groomed. When you look at her you can see it shimmer, glow and positively sparkle.

Sparkle is a black cat with white paws, and has a small white heart shape in the fur on her chest. Her big gold coloured eyes enhance her pretty face, and her perfect upright ears almost beg to hold a sparkling tiara, which should be nestled on the top of her head.

Sparkle doesn't like loud noises, and is disgusted with any untidiness around her. She ignores all signs of mess, and will just walk past it with her head held high and her nose in the air, as she looks for a clean, tidy space to sit and rest.

Her favourite place to relax, is on her fake fur-lined cat bed, which hangs on the radiator near the front window in the living room. It is warm and cosy here and always the exact temperature Sparkle enjoys. Sparkle is a very curious cat: when she climbs into this cat bed she is at the perfect height to watch everything that goes on in the room and outside the house.

Sparkle doesn't exercise very much because cleaning herself and making herself look as pretty as possible takes up most of her day. But she does go for a walk once a day, and this happens an hour before her evening meal.

Every afternoon, at 4.32pm precisely, Sparkle goes out through the cat flap in the backdoor and takes a walk around the neighbourhood. She never misses her walk because she knows how important walking is to keep her elegant figure in such good shape. She sees too many fat cats outside, and really does not want to be one of them. They are not pleasing to the eye, and Sparkle wants to please everyone who looks at her.

Sparkle takes the same route every day, except when it is raining. On rainy days she gracefully runs to a covered parking area, just over the road from where she lives, and walks around there a few times.

Sparkle doesn't like getting wet. The rain ruins her fur and makes her look like a scrawny homeless cat. She can't bear people seeing her like this and takes every precaution for it not to happen.

She never rushes her walk. She always moves at the same pace; a pace which allows her to take in her surroundings.

There is one area near her neighbourhood that Sparkle will not walk through. Here there are mean cats, cats who don't take care of themselves, and cats who are always in fights. Some of the cats have chunks bitten off their ears, others have bare patches on their bodies where clumps of fur have been pulled out. There is one very large ginger cat who lost an eye in a fight when a gang of four smaller cats all attacked him one night.

No, Sparkle does not go in this direction - EVER. These are not the type of cats she wants to be associated with.

Sparkle stays in her neighbourhood where she is very well known. When she passes the other cats who live around here, they just nod at each other, and that is as far as their communication goes …. Sparkle likes it this way.

Sparkle does not want to make friends or even have friends because she is very particular with whom she spends her time. She is far happier with her own company.

The walk always ends when Sparkle arrives back at her house and re-enters the cat flap at 5.32pm precisely. At this time her owner places a plate of freshly prepared food on her cat mat, which has her name written on it in silver letters.

Food is very important to Sparkle. She is very specific about what food she eats, and scraps from her owner's plate are a definite no no. She will only eat freshly cooked chicken or salmon, as these are the best foods to keep her coat shiny. She also insists on some bite sized luxury cat biscuits to be mixed in with the meat, as crunching on these help her white teeth stay clean and healthy.

Sparkle eats her food slowly, and savours every mouthful. She doesn't like being rushed in anything she does, and eating is something she really enjoys.

When she has finished her meal she walks up to her owner, a pretty little mature lady, and allows her to stroke her for a few minutes. When Sparkle feels she has pleased her owner enough, she moves away to find a quiet spot where she will clean herself before settling onto her cosy warm cat bed on the radiator.

Today has been a gorgeous sunny day. At 4.15pm Sparkle glances out of the window from her cat bed and is happy to see that it is perfect weather for her walk. She climbs down from her bed, allowing her elegant body to stretch for a few seconds before she walks into the kitchen.

At 4.32pm precisely, Sparkle pushes open the cat flap and gracefully jumps outside into the back garden to begin her walk.

The sun is shining and the sky is a beautiful blue as Sparkle starts walking up the road. She passes a few cats along the way and they nod politely to each other.

Sparkle enjoys her walks, and especially enjoys how good it feels to stretch her legs.

She is about half way along her usual route when suddenly the weather changes and the sky darkens. Sparkle looks around and, as she glances up, she feels something damp land on her head. There it is again …. and again ….. and again.

Shaking the drops from her face she realises it has started to rain.

OH NO …. she is going to get wet.

Sparkle panics. She can't be caught in the rain. People will see her not looking her best. That will never do.

These thoughts panic her even more and Sparkle starts to run.

She is running so fast that she isn't taking any notice of the direction she is going in.

She tries to keep her head down because it is raining even harder now. There are huge puddles forming all around and, no matter how hard she tries not to step in them, she can't miss them all.

On and on she ran with the rain falling in her eyes. She is hardly able to see where she is going, when suddenly ....

BANG!

Sparkle has run into something.

Looking up she sees she has run into a cardboard box - and the cardboard box is moving.

Sparkle watches as the flaps start to open and out peers a very angry looking cat. Its fur is long and matted and a horrid muddy colour, and its eyes look black and quite frightful.

This isn't a cat Sparkle has seen before - she knows all the cats in her neighbourhood.

The angry cat shouts, "What the #€%# do you think you are doing barging into my home like that?"

"I'm sorry," replies Sparkle. "But that's a stupid place to leave a cardboard box. And why do you call it your home?"

"What's it to you?" the angry cat spits as he climbs out of his box. "Who are you anyway? I've not seen you around here before." He slowly walks around Sparkle, looking her up and down.

Suddenly the angry cat stops walking and lets out a loud whistle.

Sparkle looks shocked and wonders what he was doing when, from seemingly out of nowhere, a lot of cats appear. They surround Sparkle and the angry cat.

"Hey guys," announces the angry cat. "Look who bumped into my home. It's that posh cat from the other neighbourhood."

Sparkle looks around at the many eyes staring at her, and she tries not to look or feel scared. "Hello," she says holding her head up and keeping her voice strong. "I seem to have gone in the wrong direction."

"Well now!" exclaims the big ginger cat with only one eye. "What shall we do with you? We don't want to waste your time," he sneers as he moves closer to Sparkle.

"How did you lose your eye?" Sparkle asks trying to take the attention away from herself.

"I was in a fight," he replies. "Do you want to fight?"

"No thank you," says Sparkle quickly as she starts to feel a little uneasy. "I have never had a fight in my life."

"Well how do you solve problems then?" asks a skinny grey cat from the crowd.

"I like to talk things through, and resolve the issue that way." says Sparkle feeling braver again. "Most things cats fight about are just difference of opinions or misunderstandings. There is never a reason to fight."

"But what about food?" another cat asks. "Do you never fight over food?"

"I have more than enough food where I live, so I don't need to fight over food." Sparkle looks around at all the cats as they listen to her. She notices they are all very skinny and do not look very healthy at all. Their fur is unkempt and their eyes do not sparkle. "Where do you all live?" she enquires.

"Anywhere we can find," replies one.

"Under a shed," cries another.

"In a doorway," a few yell together.

Sparkle is shocked at the things the cats are saying. "Do none of you have a family to live with who looks after you?"

The cats all look at each other and shake their heads.

"Would you like me to find a warm cosy home for each of you?" Sparkle asks softly.

The cats seem a little worried by this question and look over at the big ginger cat. The big ginger cat knows what is troubling them and turns towards Sparkle. "What will that entail?" he asks. "Someone tried to catch us once before and trapped some of our friends in a big net thing. We never saw them again."

"Well," Sparkle says gently, "you can all come home with me and my owner will feed you, clean you up and find homes for you. She is the kindest most loving human I know."

"Give us a minute to discuss this," says the big ginger cat as he gathers his group together.

Sparkle stands back while the cats talk. She notices that it has stopped raining and the sun is coming out again. As she looks around she can see the road which leads to her house. She must have run straight on instead of turning left, in her hurry to get home.

Being able to help these cats makes Sparkle feel good. Her life so far has been all about herself. She never had to worry about anything because everything was provided for her. She thinks she is the best cat in the world because her owner is always telling her this. But seeing these poor sad looking cats makes her view herself differently. Yes, she has everything she could ever want, but she does not feel fulfilled. Offering help to others is giving her something she didn't have before. It is giving her the feeling of a warm loving heart, pride in herself, and a purpose in life.

"Okay, we are ready to go with you," the big ginger cat says, bringing Sparkle back to the moment. "But if we are not happy then we can leave, right?"

"Yes you can," says Sparkle pleased that they trust her, "I want to help you, not scare you."

All the cats seem happy with this answer.

"Follow me," Sparkle says as she leads the way to her home.

It is quite a sight to see as Sparkle walks down the road followed by nine of the scruffiest cats in the world.

As they enter Sparkle's neighbourhood, one of the cats who lives there can't help herself and shouts out "You're being followed, Sparkle!"

Sparkle looks over and smiles, "These wonderful cats behind me are all my new friends!"

Very soon she arrives at her cat flap and invites all the cats to step through it. One at a time they cautiously go into the house, followed by Sparkle.

Sparkle's owner is getting Sparkle's food ready, and is very surprised to see so many cats coming in through the cat flap … and extremely horrified at the state of them. But then she feels sad for them and bends down to stroke them all. Some of the cats are a little hesitant of her. But eventually they all crowd around and nuzzle and brush up against her, enjoying the warmth and the comfort from her hands.

After a while the cats begin moving away from the lady and sniff around the kitchen. The lady guesses they are hungry, so she prepares something for them to eat. Soon many plates of food are placed around the kitchen floor.

And so the evening continues. The cats are bathed, much to their disgust and dislike of water; but afterwards they feel so much better. Soft blankets are laid on the floor in the kitchen, and bowls of milk and water are set down for them to freely drink whenever they feel thirsty.

Sparkle feels very pleased for her new friends, and so happy that her owner has such a big heart and is willing to help them.

None of the cats leave that night; they are all so content to have full bellies, love, warmth and comfort, which they haven't experienced before. As they settle down for the night, the sound of purring fills the kitchen.

Over the next few days, all the cats are found new homes, where they each are loved and cared for. Sparkle sees most of them as she goes on her daily walk around all the neighborhoods, making sure no other cat is in need of help.

Today Sparkle is a loving and friendly cat. She takes time to chat to every cat she sees and thinks of them all as her friends. She is a very popular cat and adored by everyone …. Sparkle likes it this way.

What would you do to help a sad, lonely, scruffy looking cat if you saw one?

How would you help a friend if they felt sad and lonely?

ARCHIE

Have you ever seen a cat who resembles an Egyptian goddess and an alien from another planet? Well, meet Archie.

Archie is a Cornish Rex, and despite his appearance, he is a very affectionate and friendly cat who likes to have fun and frolic about.

He has soft, wavy hair, an egg-shaped face, large ears and long legs. He is extremely active, agile and fast. His green eyes see everything that moves, and what he can't see, his very sensitive nose can spot. He can jump the highest fence and climb the tallest tree with no problem at all, and he can lift almost his own body weight in his mouth.

Archie is a highly intelligent cat, and well known by the animals in his neighborhood for being very good at helping with problems.

This morning Archie wakes up feeling excited for the day ahead. He sees the sun shining in through the window and hears his owner making breakfast. He stands up and stretches, then gives himself a quick wash with his paws. His owner calls him, so he runs into the kitchen where he is scooped up for a cuddle. Archie likes to snuggle with his owner and enjoys the affection he receives.

Back on the ground, Archie gobbles up his bowl of food. Now he's ready for the day ahead and jumps through the cat flap, taking a deep breath as he looks around at the beautiful day. He listens to the birds singing sweetly while he thinks about where he will go to explore; there are not many places he doesn't know about around here.

Archie decides to go for a run in the nearby field, and sets off just as a bird flies really low over him. It's a sparrow, and Archie tries to move out of its way, but it keeps flying straight at him. Archie stops and looks up at the sparrow, who is now hovering a little way above his head.

"At last I have your attention," the sparrow squawks at Archie.

"That's a strange way to get my attention," says Archie, a little annoyed. "What do you want?"

The sparrow perches on a fence close to where Archie is standing. "I've been told by the wise old owl that you are very good at solving problems."

Archie looks at the sparrow as he says, "I have been known to, yes."

"Well I have a problem I need help with," the sparrow quickly announces, now that she has Archie's full attention. "Someone keeps stealing the eggs out of my nest. When I leave the nest to get some food for myself, an egg disappears. I started with four eggs and now I only have one left. Can you please help me?"

Archie is looking forward to his run but he doesn't like seeing this sparrow upset, so he replies, "Yes, I'll do my best. Take me to your nest and I will see how I can help you."

The sparrow flies off to the tree where her nest is, and Archie runs along trying to keep up with her.

The sparrow lands on her nest and sounds relieved as she says, "My last egg is still here."

Archie looks around and decides on a plan. "I will climb up into this tree, next to your tree, and lie on one of the branches to wait for whoever is taking your eggs. Now, give me a few minutes to get settled, and then you fly off and find some food. Don't worry, we will catch whoever is doing this."

The sparrow agrees to the plan and settles on her nest while Archie gets into position.

Archie climbs the tree. He chooses a good strong branch to lie on, which is the same distance from the ground as the branch the sparrow's nest is on in the opposite tree. Then he lies flat against the branch, with enough leaves covering him so he is not too visible. When he feels comfortable, he stays perfectly still, ready for action.

A few minutes later the sparrow flies off.

Archie does not move a muscle … he just waits …. and waits …. and waits.

Then he hears something nearby.

He can't turn his head to look because he has to keep as still as possible, so as not to scare the thief.

But the noise soon stops.

Archie waits again.

It isn't long before he sees the thief.

A blackbird flies towards the tree and lands on the edge of the sparrow's nest. He looks around and then bends his head into the nest. As quick as a flash, Archie jumps from his tree, leaps onto the blackbird and grabs him in his mouth. Then as swiftly as he can, he jumps out of the tree and lands on the ground, still holding the blackbird in his beak.

"Ouch! You're hurting me," squeals the blackbird, trying to wiggle out of Archie's mouth. "Put me down. NOW!"

"Not until you tell me why you are taking the sparrow's eggs," Archie says firmly.

The blackbird stops wiggling.

"Well, I'm waiting," says Archie.

"I can't tell you because you'll laugh at me," whispers the blackbird.

"I promise I won't laugh at you. Just be honest with me," replies Archie gently.

"Well, it's because," the blackbird hesitates for a minute before he continues. "It's because I can't lay eggs, and I really want to be a daddy bird. So

I take other birds' eggs and sit on them until they hatch."

"But you have already taken three of the sparrow's eggs. They can't all have hatched already," Archie says, surprised by the blackbirds reply.

"No they haven't," says the blackbird quietly. "I dropped them on the way to my nest. I can be a little clumsy at times."

"You have made the sparrow very unhappy." Archie tries to sound cross.

"Oh I'm sorry. That was not my intention. I am really a very nice bird," replies the blackbird as he starts to wiggle again. "Can you put me down now, please? I promise I won't go anywhere."

Archie opens his mouth, and the blackbird lands on the ground. He stands up and flaps his wings a little, and then looks at Archie and asks, "What do you suggest I do now?"

Archie looks at the blackbird and says, "I've always found that being honest is the best way forward, and I feel so much better when I speak from my heart."

"I like that," says the sparrow thoughtfully.

"Here's a suggestion," Archie offers. "Why don't you make friends with the sparrow and ask if you can watch her egg while she goes for food and has a little exercise."

"That sounds like a great idea," the blackbird says as he flaps his wings again. "Then I can be a kind of uncle to the little bird when it hatches."

"I like your thinking," says Archie, watching the sparrow fly back to her nest. "Now's your chance to go and say sorry, and ask her to forgive you."

The blackbird looks up at the sparrow. Before he goes, he says to Archie, "Thank you for making me see sense. I feel so much happier now. I'm going to talk to the sparrow and hope she allows me to be part of her family."

Archie watches as the blackbird flies up into the tree and lands on the branch, a little way from the sparrow's nest.

The blackbird apologises and explains why he has stolen the eggs. At first the sparrow turns her back on him, but after she listens for a while she turns and faces him. Before long the blackbird is sitting next to the nest, and Archie knows the sparrow forgives him.

Happy with the outcome, Archie starts back on his run to the field.

A few minutes later he stands at the edge of the field. The grass is long in places, and the only way Archie can get through it is to jump like a sheep. This is a different kind of exercise to what he had in mind, but it is fun.

"Hey watch out, dimwit, you nearly trod on me!" says a little squeaky voice. Archie looks down and sees a tiny mouse holding back a blade of grass.

"Sorry, I didn't see you there," Archie apologises. "You are so tiny and this grass is so long."

"Well, now that you're here, maybe you can help me," the tiny mouse says, looking up at Archie. "I'm trying to find my brother. We were running through this grass, trying to get back to our mouse-hole, when I suddenly realised he wasn't behind me anymore. I've been walking around for ages looking for him with no luck. Can you help me find him, please?"

Archie looks at the tiny mouse and decides to go for a run another day. Helping someone in distress is far more important. And he replies, "Yes, I'll do my best. Which direction shall we go in first?"

"Let's go this way," says the tiny mouse, pointing to her right.

"Why don't you climb upon my head and then we can go faster, and I won't step on you," Archie suggests.

"Okay," agrees the tiny mouse, climbing upon Archie until she reaches the top of his head. She holds onto his ears with her paws, and Archie starts walking.

They walk for a few minutes and eventually come to the edge of the field without seeing any sign of the tiny mouse's brother.

"Let's go back into the grass and zig zag across this time," suggests Archie.

"Yes, let's give that a try," agrees the tiny mouse. "This field is so big I'm worried we won't find my brother at all."

"Don't worry," Archie says, trying to reassure her. "I have a good feeling that everything is going to be all right. Stay positive. When you feel positive deep inside of you, only good things can happen. Try thinking about how happy you will feel when we find your brother."

Archie starts walking back into the tall grass, and the tiny mouse thinks about her brother.

A few minutes pass, and then, without warning, the tiny mouse starts to pull on Archie's ears and yells, "STOP. STOP. I see him. He's lying over there."

Archie sees him and hurries over. The mouse has been caught in a mousetrap and seems to be unconscious.

The tiny mouse climbs down from Archie's head and runs over to her brother.

She leans over him. "He's still breathing," she says. "I can feel his breath on my cheek. Quickly, can you help me open the mouse trap and release him?"

Archie looks at the poor mouse caught in the trap. It is a spring trap and the bar is lying across his belly, and a piece of cheese is not far from his mouth. He must have stepped on the wooden floor of the trap to get the cheese and knocked the spring which pushed the bar down on him.

"Right, we need to make a plan," Archie says, thinking quickly. "You hold onto one of your brother's legs, and I will lift the bar of the trap. As soon as I do that, you have no time to waste. You must pull your brother, with all your strength, away from the trap immediately, otherwise the spring will trap him again. We only have one chance at this - he may not survive another hit with that bar."

"Okay," says the tiny mouse. She grabs one of her brother's legs tightly with her paws, and declares, "I can do this."

Archie gets into position with his paw under the bar. "I will count to three and then I will lift the bar off him."

"One …. two …. THREE."

And Archie lifts the bar back, and at the same time the tiny mouse pulls her brother away from the trap with all her strength.

Archie lets the bar go, and it snaps down onto the wooden board where the mouse had been lying.

"Nice work," says Archie to the tiny mouse. He looks over to where the two mice are nestled in the grass. "How's your brother doing?" he asks quietly, walking over to them.

The tiny mouse is tenderly rocking her brother in her arms. "He's very cold," she whispers. Archie pushes some blades of grass over the mouse to help him get warm.

"It's the shock of being snapped in the mouse trap that has made him cold," Archie replies.

The tiny mouse continues rocking her brother and telling him how much she loves him.

All of a sudden, the mouse starts to stir, and opens his eyes. The first thing he sees is Archie starring down at him. He clings to his sister and looks terrified.

"It's all right," she says gently. "Archie is a friend and helped me find you. He's not going to hurt us …. are you?" she suddenly asks, looking up at Archie.

"No, I'm not going to hurt you," Archie says, smiling. "I want to see you both happy and well."

The tiny mouse smiles back, and her brother relaxes in her arms. "Thank you for helping us," she says, "and for your advice about staying positive, it really did work. I will remember that in future."

"Is there anything else I can do before I leave?" Archie asks.

"No, you have done more than enough for us," replies the tiny mouse gratefully. "We will sit here for a while until my brother feels fully rested. Thank you again."

"My pleasure," says Archie. "I'm glad I could help. Now take care and bye for now."

As Archie jumps through the long grass, he thinks what a great day he is having, helping others solve their problems.

Eventually he comes to the edge of the field and decides to go home and rest for a while. Jumping through long grass is much more tiring than running.

Archie starts walking back to his house when all of a sudden, a bird flies quite close over his head again. He looks up and sees the sparrow he had helped earlier.

"The blackbird is looking after my egg while I stretch my wings," she says as she circles above Archie. "Thank you for helping me today. I think the blackbird will be a good friend to me and my family."

"That's great news," says Archie. "I'm so pleased for you all."

"Enjoy your walk," says the sparrow as she flies off up into the blue sky.

Helping others really makes Archie feel happy inside. No matter what problems others have, he always manages to find a solution for them.

Archie enters his home through the cat flap, just as his owner puts a saucer of cold creamy milk down for him. He takes a refreshing drink and then finds a sunny spot to lie down. Tomorrow he will go for a run in the nearby field. But now it's time to take a well deserved nap.

Do you think you can solve problems as well as Archie does?

TOMMY

Tommy loves going for walks with his humans. They don't actually take him for a walk, he just tags along with them when they go out of their front door. Their walks are always to the park, which is just up the road and round the corner from where they live.

Tommy is a ginger tabby cat. His body is long and slender, with a beautiful pale orange colour fur. When he walks, his steps are precise and dainty for a boy cat. He is a very affectionate cat and devoted to his humans. He loves them unconditionally and always wants to be with them.

When his humans are not home, he spends most of the day indoors sleeping, curled up on one of the human's beds. He doesn't mind which bed he sleeps on because they are all soft and comfortable.

He waits for the humans to go out and then he jumps upon his chosen bed, on the covers up against the pillows. Then, he walks around in many tiny circles until he feels the spot is just right. Only then will he lie down and peacefully sleep until his humans come home.

Tommy doesn't know where the humans go, but he knows that when he wakes up, they will be home. The noise they make coming into the house always wakes him, as they are not quiet humans at all!

Most mornings Tommy follows his humans around the house, while they go from room to room doing things and making noises. Sometimes they stop what they are doing and stroke him, but most mornings they seem to be in a rush and will just ignore him.

When they are finished going from room to room, they go downstairs and have some food. If Tommy stands by his bowl, which is on the floor by the back door, one of the humans puts some of his food in it for him.

Tommy likes to sit next to the little humans while they eat, because they feed him some of their food. Actually, he doesn't sit next to the little humans, he sits on the table next to their plate of food. However, if one of the big humans sees him on the table, they shout and push him off onto the floor. But Tommy doesn't care, he just waits until they are not looking and jumps back up onto the table again. The little humans think this is very funny and laugh out loud, and give him more of their food.

Most days after the humans have eaten, they go out of the front door together. Tommy always follows them. Sometimes they get into their car and Tommy knows that this means they will be gone for a while. When this happens he goes back in the house through the cat flap, up the stairs and chooses which comfy bed he is going to sleep on, and stays there until they come home.

Today Tommy follows his humans as he does everyday. They do not seem to be in their usual hurry, so he knows that they could be staying home with him.

The humans sit around after they eat their food, and the little humans play with Tommy when he walks over and rubs against them. He loves their cuddles and attention and he purrs loudly to show his appreciation.

Sometime later in the day the humans start getting ready to go out. Tommy follows them around the house and eventually they go out of the front door.

Today they don't get into their car. Instead, they walk past the car and up the road, which leads to the park. They don't go to the park very often, but when they do, Tommy enjoys going along with them and watching the little humans play.

The humans walk up the road and Tommy follows a little way behind them. Then, at the top of the road, instead of turning left to go to the park as they had always done before, they turn right and walk along this new road.

Tommy has never been down this road before.

Where are they going?

Tommy has no idea, but follows his humans anyway.

They walk down the road, turn left and then right, continuing to walk past a new park the little humans seem excited about, and soon afterwards they stop at a really busy road.

Tommy has never seen such a busy road, so he creeps into a garden close by. He sits beside a bush where he can just about keep an eye on what is going on.

The humans stand on the curb near the busy road and keep looking left and right, and the cars keep zooming past them. Eventually the big human shouts something in a very firm and loud voice, and they all start walking quickly across the busy road.

Tommy runs out from the garden towards the busy road. He wants to go with them. But then he hears his humans calling his name and holding their hands up, shouting, "NO! STAY THERE!"

Tommy stops at the curb just as six cars go by, each of them going really fast. The noise the cars make frightens him.

The next thing he hears is his humans telling him he is a good boy. Then they wave at him and continue walking up the road ahead of them.

Tommy watches them go, feeling upset as he is unable to follow because more cars are coming along this busy road. One car goes past and beeps its horn really loudly, which makes Tommy jump.

He doesn't like this busy road. The roads near his house are virtually quiet compared to this one, with only a few cars going by now and again.

Tommy moves back from the curb and goes to sit in the garden by the bush.

What should he do now?

He likes going for a walk with his humans but crossing this busy road is far too scary.

Tommy is in deep thought when he hears a rustling sound nearby. He looks over and sees a big blackbird using his beak to search for something in the old dead leaves on the ground.

"Hey, what are you looking for?" Tommy asks the blackbird.

"I'm looking for worms to eat. I'm feeling a little peckish," replies the blackbird as he hops closer to Tommy. "What are you doing?"

"I'm waiting for my humans to come back," says Tommy. "They crossed over that busy road there and now I can't follow them."

The blackbird looks over at the busy road. "Why not?" he asks.

"There are too many fast cars going by, and I'm scared they may hit me," Tommy says, looking really sad.

"Can't you fly over the road?" the blackbird asks, trying to help.

"I'm a cat, not a bird," laughs Tommy. "I don't have wings."

"Oh yes, I see that now," the blackbird says as he studies Tommy a little closer. "Well maybe you should just sit here and wait for them to come back. I have to go now. There are no worms under these leaves so I must look somewhere else." And he flies off without even saying goodbye!

Tommy watches the big blackbird fly away and then hears a squeaking noise close by him. He looks down and sees a tiny grey mouse sitting next to his paws.

"What are you looking at?" the mouse squeaks at Tommy.

"The big blackbird who was here a minute ago," Tommy replies.

The mouse runs around Tommy a few times. He runs so quickly that Tommy feels dizzy trying to watch him.

Coming to a halt in front of Tommy, the mouse says, "Are you doing anything fun today?"

"No," replies Tommy sadly. "I was walking with my humans until they crossed that busy road. I'm too scared to cross it because there are so many fast cars. So I'm just sitting here waiting until they return."

The mouse starts running around Tommy again. "Why don't you just run across the road really fast like me; then the cars won't get you."

"I'm a cat, not a mouse and I can't run as fast as you," Tommy says laughing. "You are tiny and move like grease lightening. I doubt there's much that will catch you. Unfortunately, I am a lot bigger than you and cannot go as fast."

"Oh yes, I see that now," the mouse says as he studies Tommy a little closer. "Well maybe you should just sit here and wait for them to come back. I have to go now. Life is always busy." And he is gone in a flash, without even saying goodbye!

"What are you doing in my garden?" a big gruff voice says behind Tommy.

Tommy turns around slowly, unsure of who or what this frightening voice belongs to.

He comes face to face with a little brown dog. Not what he was expecting at all.

"You sound really scary," says Tommy laughing, "but you are only a little dog."

"Yes," says the dog, "isn't that funny! I like tricking people into thinking I am a big ferocious beast. Anyway, I've been watching you sit here for a while now. What are you waiting for?"

Again Tommy repeats his story and then says, "So all I can do now is wait for them to return."

After the little dog thinks about Tommy's difficult situation for a moment, he says, "Why don't you just walk slowly out into the road. When I do that, all the cars slow down and stop for me. When they stop for you, you can then continue to cross the road and go and find your humans"

"I'm a cat, not a dog," says Tommy, feeling he is getting nowhere with the help from his new friends. "When I step into the road the cars just beep their horns at me and carry on driving."

"Oh yes, I see that now," the little dog says as he studies Tommy a little closer. "Well maybe you should just sit here and wait for them to come back. I have to go now. It's time for my dinner." And he walks off without even saying goodbye!

It is starting to get dark, and Tommy is feeling a little tired. He has been sitting in this garden for ages and he hasn't had his nap today.

"What am I going to do?" he says to himself, as he watches the cars go racing by.

"What are you going to do about what?" asks a gentle voice.

Tommy turns around and sees a big fluffy white Persian cat slowly walking towards him.

"I see you are watching the cars," the Persian cat says as she sits down beside Tommy. "You don't want to go near that busy road. My sister tried to cross it last week and was knocked over by a speeding car; she still hasn't recovered properly."

"I'm sorry to hear that," Tommy says. "I was following my humans and they crossed that busy road and told me to stay here. I love going for walks with them but I'm scared of the cars."

"Well my advice to you is to stay here and wait." the Persian cat says reassuringly. "Humans have a tendency of walking back the same way as they went."

"Thank you," Tommy replies, feeling a little happier with this advice.

"We cats understand each other," the Persian cat continues, "and know how to follow our instincts. If something doesn't feel right, then we shouldn't do it. When we wait patiently, good things can happen."

The Persian cat stands up and stretches her elegant body. "I have a feeling your humans won't be too much longer. Enjoy your time relaxing in this pretty garden. Goodbye."

"Goodbye," says Tommy, and he watches the Persian cat walk slowly and gracefully away.

Suddenly, Tommy hears his name being called.

He looks over in the direction of the busy road, and there he sees his humans walking back down the road they had walked up earlier. They stop at the curb and wait until there are no cars, and then cross the road.

Tommy runs over to meet them, and they are all excited to see him. The little humans bend down and stroke him, and Tommy walks around each one of them purring loudly.

The big human starts walking and calls to the little humans, "Come on, let's go home. You must all be hungry because it's time for tea!"

Tommy realises that he feels really hungry too, and follows his humans home, thankful that they are all back together again.

Do you like going for walks with your family?
Where is your favourite place to walk?

THE THREE AMIGOS

Casey loves nothing more than sitting with Dad in front of the television, as they watch the ball game together. Casey starts off on Dad's lap, and gradually moves to the large arm of the chair when Dad becomes more vocal as the game goes on. When Dad cheers for his team, Casey raises his head, knowing that he will get it rubbed, as Dad says this brings the team good luck.

Casey is a very friendly Birman cat, with long silky hair, deep sapphire blue eyes, and white socks on each paw. His body is a pale cream colour, while his face, ears and tail are a dark chocolate brown colour.

You may think that Casey is an unusual breed, but so are his brother and sister. Although they are not true brothers and sister, they have lived together long enough to feel like they are. Their mum and dad call them The Three Amigos because they love being together and seem to know what each other is thinking.

Charlie, the eldest of the three cats, is a Ragamuffin breed. His extremely thick fur is a blend of white and pale grey colours. He has a gentle nature and worries about everyone all the time. Being the eldest, his brother and sister listen to him and do what he tells them, without question. But most importantly, Charlie loves his mum. He will sit on her lap all day long if he can, and wherever she goes, he goes too.

Sammi is the youngest of the three, and is a very sweet and caring cat. She is a Snowshoe breed with black and white fur. Sammi spends most of the day lying on her cat size four poster bed, which is placed in a perfect spot in the living room so she can see exactly what is going on.

The Three Amigos may sound like very unusual breeds, but they really are just ordinary cats, like the cats you and I have, and the cats we see around us everyday ..... or are they?

The Three Amigos are house cats and live with their owners on the third floor of an apartment block, which has a nice balcony where they can enjoy the outdoors together. Because they are so high up, the cats are only allowed on the balcony when an adult is with them, in case they accidentally fall from the great height.

This really only applies to Casey, who loves to climb. He climbs on the counter in the kitchen, especially when food is being prepared, and tries to climb the curtains to catch flies. But his favourite place to climb is in the bathroom. In here, he climbs onto the counter and then swings to the ground from the light cord … and repeats over and over again, until Dad comes and scolds him, as he's afraid Casey may hurt himself.

Today Dad is not watching the ball game on the television; instead he is going to the game with his friends. Casey watches him getting ready, and when he hears him shout, "See you later guys!"

as he shuts the front door, Casey runs out to the balcony, where Mum is sitting, doing her crocheting. Casey watches as Dad comes out of the building and walks along the path until he disappears from view.

"He'll be back soon, Casey," says Charlie from Mum's lap.

"I know," replies Casey sadly, "but I enjoy watching the game with him."

"Come and play ball with me," suggests Sammi, who is knocking a small rubber ball around the legs of the furniture on the balcony.

"I'm okay sitting here, thanks," Casey says, not wanting to take his eyes off the spot he last saw Dad.

Charlie nestles into Mum's lap, getting his front paws slightly caught up in her yarn.

"Sorry, Charlie," says Mum suddenly, "I don't feel too good. I need to go and lie down for a while." She gathers her crocheting together and places it in a bag as she stands up and goes into the living room. "Come on kitties," she says, turning to her pets. "Come inside. I don't like you out on the balcony by yourselves."

The three cats reluctantly come into the living room, and Mum closes the door behind them. Then she goes into the bedroom and lies down on the bed, just as Charlie jumps up to be with her. Mum closes her eyes and Charlie moves up to her chest and gently rubs her with his paw.

"That feels good," Mum says, stroking Charlie's head. "You are such a comforting boy."

Within minutes, Mum falls asleep and Charlie lies beside her, watching her breathe.

After a while, Mum's breathing pattern changes and Charlie starts to worry. Mum becomes really hot and Charlie feels sure something is wrong.

He jumps off the bed and runs to the lounge, where Casey and Sammi are resting.

"There's something wrong with Mum," he says in a panic. "We need to get Dad as fast as we can."

"But Dad's out," says Casey, unsure of what to do.

"Someone has to go and find him," says Charlie. "Mum needs him. I can't go because I have to be with her. Sort something out guys; I'm trusting you to do this." And he turns and goes back to the bedroom, as fast as he can.

"What shall we do, Casey?" asks Sammi.

"I don't know," says Casey. "You're the clever one; you think of something."

Sammi thinks for a moment and then says, "I think you should climb down from the balcony and head along the path Dad walked and find him."

"The balcony is awfully high," says Casey, feeling a little worried with this plan. "I don't think I can do that."

"Let's go and take a look," suggests Sammi. "Maybe there's something you can use to help you climb down."

The two cats move to go out on the balcony and then remember the door is closed.

"How are we going to get out there?" asks Casey, looking up at the door handle.

"I'll get Charlie," says Sammi. "He's good at opening doors. He always manages to open the bathroom door when Mum is in there."

Sammi runs into the bedroom and looks up at the bed. "Charlie," she whispers, "we can't open the door to the balcony. Can you come and help, please?"

Charlie looks at Mum, who is still sleeping. Carefully, so as not to wake her, he jumps off the bed and runs to the balcony door.

"How's she doing?" asks Sammi, running behind him.

"Her breathing sounds really strange," Charlie replies, as he jumps up at the handle on the door.

Hey presto ... the door flies open.

"Okay," says Charlie, "I don't know your plan but good luck with it ... and please hurry." And he runs back to be with Mum.

Casey and Sammi go out onto the balcony.

"Right," says Sammi, "let's look for something we can use to lower you to the ground."

The cats search all around but with no luck.

"I can't see anything," says Casey.

"Neither can I," says Sammi, feeling frustrated and wondering what to do next. "This is taking too long, Casey; what else can we do?" she asks, as she notices her little rubber ball by one of the chairs. Frustrated, she flicks the ball under the chair.

The ball bounces against something, and immediately rolls back out.

"What's under there?" asks Casey, as Sammi crawls under the chair to take a look.

Within seconds, she crawls back out … with something in her mouth, and drops it on the floor.

"It's some rope Dad must have used for something," says Sammi. "He's normally so tidy, and always puts everything away."

"Well, I'm glad he missed putting this rope away," says Casey. "It's just what we need."

"Help me lift it up onto the wall," says Sammi.

Together, the cats lift the rope onto the wall. Luckily there is a big knot at one end of the rope, which fits nice and tightly into a hook Mum uses to hang flower pots from.

After fixing the rope knot securely into the hook, the cats push the rest of the rope over the wall.

"Ok, Casey," says Sammi, looking over at her brother. "It's ready for you."

Casey looks down at the ground. "I don't think I can do this Sammi. I'm scared," he murmurs. "We are so high up here."

"Casey, you have to," Sammi says gently. "Mum needs you to do this. Take a deep breath and don't think about how high up we are. Pretend you are swinging on the light cord in the bathroom. I know you can do this. Please, Casey, go and find Dad."

"Go and find Dad," Casey whispers to himself. "Dad always makes everything better." And with that thought in his head, he grabs the rope between his paws and lowers himself to the ground.

Sammi watches him land and cheers loudly. "I knew you could do it, Casey!" she shouts. "Now, GO AND FIND DAD."

"Thanks, Sammi, I will," Casey shouts back, and he runs up the road as fast as he can.

Sammi goes into the bedroom and says to Charlie, as quietly as she can, "Casey is on his way to get Dad."

Charlie did not reply; he is too concerned about the strange noises mum is making.

"She'll be okay, Charlie; I'm sure she will. Our mum's tough; nothing keeps her down for long," Sammi says trying not to feel worried herself.

"I hope so, Sammi," whispers Charlie, as he snuggles closer to mum.

Casey runs up the road, not really knowing where he is going, but determined to find Dad. The road is long and soon he comes to a crossroads. He stops running and sits by the curb to catch his breath; being a house cat, he is only used to running inside the apartment.

Looking up and down the different roads, he wonders which way to go next.

"Hey Casey, what are you doing out here?" asks a familiar voice.

Casey turns around and sees Dad walking towards him. Casey is so pleased to see him, but knowing he doesn't have time to waste, he turns and runs back down the road he has just come from.

Dad realises something must be wrong because Casey didn't even go up to him to say hello. But while he wonders what this could be, he also wonders why his cat is outside, and how did he manage to get out?

Seeing Casey is already half way up the road, Dad senses the need to hurry. So, without wasting another second, he runs after his cat.

Arriving back at the apartment block, Casey looks round just as Dad catches up with him. Dad sees the rope hanging down from his balcony and, looking at Casey, he says, "Is that how you got down? What is happening up there, Casey? Did Mum send you? Is she okay?"

Feeling the panic rising inside of him, Dad rushes to the main door, puts in the code and goes inside, with Casey following behind. They quickly walk to the lift and go up to the third floor.

Outside his front door, Dad uses the key to open it and steps inside … expecting the worst.

But all is quiet.

Dad walks into the lounge, but no one is there.

The door to the balcony is open, but no one is out there.

He hurries along the hallway to the bedroom, just as Mum starts to stir. Charlie is lying next to her, and lifts his head to see if she is okay. Sammi, who had been asleep curled up on the floor at the foot of the bed, hears Dad coming into the bedroom and wakes up, just as Casey sits down beside her.

Dad sits on the bed as Mum opens her eyes and yawns. "Hello, Love," she says, stretching herself. "How was the game?"

"It was very good, and we won," he replies, as he strokes Charlie's head. "Then a strange thing happened on the way home. I was met by Casey."

"Oh, how did he get out?" asks Mum, looking worried. "Is he okay?"

"Yes, he's fine," Dad says, as Casey jumps onto his lap. "I think he climbed down the balcony using a rope."

"That can't be possible," says Mum, reaching over and stroking Casey. "I shut the door to the balcony before I came to bed, and where would he get a rope from?"

"Well, the door is open now and a rope is hanging down from the balcony. I guess we will never really know what happened," says Dad glancing at the three cats in turn. "But when I saw Casey, I thought something was wrong here. Are you okay?"

"I'm fine now," replies Mum, sitting up on the bed. "Although I did feel a little strange earlier. That's why I came in here to lie down. I expect this all has something to do with Charlie; you know how he worries about me."

Hearing his name, Charlie moves up closer to Mum, and she hugs him tightly to her.

"Are you feeling better now?" Dad asks, looking lovingly at his wife.

"Yes, I am," says Mum, taking Dad's hand to reassure him. "Shall I make us a cup of tea? I'm feeling quite thirsty."

Squeezing Mum's hand, Dad says, "No, you stay there for a while longer and I'll make the tea." He places Casey onto the bed then goes into the kitchen to put the kettle on.

"Okay," says Mum. "But I must go to the loo first," and she gets up from the bed and heads to the bathroom.

"I'm so pleased Mum's feeling better," says Charlie. "Thanks you two, for getting Dad. I'm sorry for panicking and causing unnecessary alarm."

"That's okay," says Casey. "We can't take any chances where Mum and Dad are concerned; we would be lost without them."

"I agree," says Sammi, jumping up onto the bed to be with the others. "Casey did a great job of climbing down the rope to the ground. He is a real super hero."

"It was nothing," says Casey, feeling just a little pleased with Sammi's praise. "We figured things out together and we all did our bit. It was team work!"

"That's why we're called The Three Amigos," Charlie says. "We are always there for each other, no matter what, and ready to take action."

"Yes, we are!" agree Casey and Sammi.

"The Three Amigos!" they shout together.

And feeling happy that the day ended so well, they curl up together on the bed, and promptly fall asleep.

The Three Amigos worked well with each other. Could you solve a problem with the help of your best friends?

Dear Reader

I hope you have enjoyed reading my stories as much as I enjoyed writing them. I would love to hear your replies to some of the questions I asked throughout this book; either send me an email or write on my instagram page. You are also welcome to send me suggestions for future books you would like me to write.

Smiles and hugs

Jacqueline

email: mytranquilspirits@gmail.com
instagram: @grandma_has_a _story
podcast: Grandma Has A Story

Made in the USA
Monee, IL
27 October 2020